D1208445

The Tasha Tudor Book of Fairy Tales

Selected, Edited and Illustrated by TASHA TUDOR

PLATT & MUNK, *Publishers*
A Division of Grosset & Dunlap
NEW YORK

Foreword

FAIRY TALES are perennially the favorite literature of childhood. They can be traced back, in the form we know, at least to 1697, when Charles Perrault's book, *Contes de Ma Mère l'Oie* (Tales of Mother Goose) was first published. Perrault's tales are still read and told today, and two of them are included in this book.

Children deserve, indeed require, the special charm and imagery of the fanciful. It is for their particular delight that this edition is published. No other collection of fairy tales published this century has quite caught so fully the classical simplicity, warmth and magic of fairy stories as has *The Tasha Tudor Book of Fairy Tales.*

For this book is far more than a collection of favorite stories illustrated by a favorite artist, although it is that as well. These are the stories that Tasha Tudor loved as a child and has told to her children. She has selected them, edited and shaped them, and with her own unerring taste has illustrated them with affectionate care and delicate grace.

Here are represented the master storytellers, Perrault, Hans Christian Andersen and the Brothers Grimm, as well as folk tales from old Russia and the English. These stories, newly retold, blend wit and sparkle and soaring imagination with the delightful artistry of Tasha Tudor, who sees beauty and magic in everyday things of the house, the woods and the fields, and weaves them all skillfully into her interpretations.

Throughout, *The Tasha Tudor Book of Fairy Tales* is distinguished for its expansiveness of spirit and feeling and its elegance of design and color.

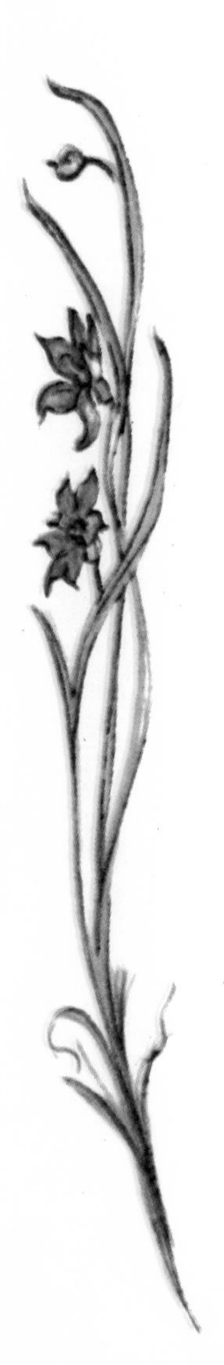

Made in the United States of America.
Library of Congress Catalog Card Number: 61-13221
ISBN 0-448-44200-0 (Trade Edition)
ISBN 0-448-13036-X (Library Edition)

Contents

T. Tudor

Thumbelina

ONCE THERE WAS a woman who wanted to have a little child more than anything else in the world, so she went to see a wise old witch and asked her advice.

"Ah," said the old witch. "That is very simple. Here," and she took from her pocket a strange-looking barleycorn. "Plant this in a flowerpot when you get home, and see what springs up from it."

"Many thanks," said the woman, and gave the witch a coin.

As soon as she got home, she planted the barleycorn, and in a few days a green shoot came up and grew into a sturdy plant, much like a tulip. The blossom was tightly closed.

Pleased with her pretty plant, the woman kissed the bud. It sprang open at her touch, and there sat a lovely little girl child. She was no bigger than your thumb, so she was called Thumbelina.

She was given a polished walnut shell for a cradle, violet petals for a mattress, and a rose leaf for a counterpane. During the day the woman placed a plate filled with water on the table and surrounded it with flowers. Here Thumbelina sailed about on a tulip leaf or played among the flowers.

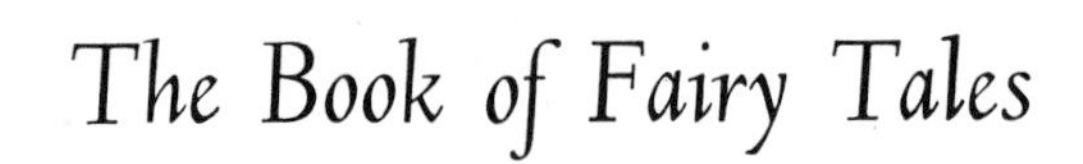

Then one night a dreadful thing happened. An old mother toad, living at the bottom of the garden, hopped in the open window and stole little Thumbelina! She lifted the walnut shell and carried the child, sound asleep in her tiny bed, to the muddy stream where she lived with her ugly son.

"See the lovely bride I've brought you," she said to him. "You can marry her as soon as we get the house ready for you to live in."

While they were preparing the bridal bower deep in the mud, they put Thumbelina, still asleep in her bed, on a lily pad in the stream. When she awoke in the morning she was frightened to find herself surrounded by deep water, floating on a lily pad far out in a great swift stream.

She had no sooner climbed out of her tiny bed than the old toad appeared, bringing her ugly son. "Let me introduce your future husband to you, pretty child," she said. But all the future husband could do was to stare and mutter, "Koax, koax." Then he and his mother took the walnut shell and disappeared with it into the mud, leaving Thumbelina alone on the lily pad.

"Oh, how can I ever marry that horrid, horrid toad?" wept the tiny girl.

The little fish in the stream heard her crying and took pity on her. They gathered around the stem of the lily pad, nibbling at it until they had cut it through. It floated free, carrying Thumbelina away where the toad could not follow. All the birds in the bushes beside the stream sang, "What a pretty little maid!" as she floated by.

Then a white butterfly alighted by her. She tied one end of her scarf to its body and the other end to the lily pad, and it drew her swiftly along.

All would have been well if a June bug had not spied Thumbelina floating on the lily pad. He swooped down and carried her to a high tree.

Thumbelina

The other beetles in the tree did not think the tiny girl was at all pretty. "Ugh! She is not even shaped like a beetle!" screamed the lady June bugs. "How ugly she is with only two legs and no feelers! Let's get rid of her!"

So the June bug who had first found her carried her down and put her on a daisy plant, and poor Thumbelina was left alone. All summer she lived there. She ate honey out of the flowers, and drank the dew from the grass. At night she slept beneath a great dock leaf that sheltered her from the rain.

Summer passed and autumn's bright colors made way for winter. Now Thumbelina, in rags, wandered through the dry stalks of a cornfield, to her a huge forest.

At last, cold and weary, she came to the house of a little fieldmouse, deep in the stubble. The fieldmouse made her welcome, saying, "Keep my house neat and tell me stories of the outside world, and we shall get on well."

Then the fieldmouse's neighbor, the mole, came calling. Thumbelina did not like him in spite of his fine velvet coat, for he hated sunshine and birds and flowers. But he had fallen in love with Thumbelina, and soon he and the fieldmouse were busy planning the wedding—for the fieldmouse was a born matchmaker.

One cold day the mole took the ladies walking through the big passage he had dug between their home and his. On the floor lay a dead swallow that had fallen through a hole in the roof that morning.

"Silly things, these birds," muttered the mole. "All they can do is twitter and sing. Then they freeze in the first cold wind and clutter up my passage-way!" He kicked the bird and thumped the roof with his walking cane to make sure he had mended the hole properly.

But later Thumbelina returned with bits of hay and milkweed down, which she tucked around the swallow, stopping now and then to kiss his

soft feathers. Soon to her great joy the bird opened his eyes and spoke to her in a weak voice. He was not dead at all, but had fainted from the cold. His companions had flown to warmer countries, and he had stayed behind.

All winter the little girl cared for the wounded bird, and when the spring arrived she carefully opened the hole in the roof again, so that he could fly out into the sunshine and be free.

"You have been kind to me," said the swallow. "Let me take you with me out of the darkness into the green wood."

But Thumbelina knew it would be unkind to leave the fieldmouse who had given her shelter, so she could only shake her head and watch the happy bird go flying up into the blue sky.

But now the fieldmouse grew cross because Thumbelina showed no interest in the beautiful trousseau she was planning. Four spiders were engaged to spin, and Thumbelina herself was set to spinning and weaving night and day, making the delicate garments. The summer passed and then the fieldmouse said, "In four weeks' time you shall be married, and lucky indeed you are to get so fine a husband as our good neighbor, the mole! Stop crying or I'll bite you to teach you a lesson in gratitude!"

The wedding day arrived. In despair, Thumbelina stepped out into the sunshine for a moment and threw her arms around a red flower growing at the doorstep. "Dear flower," she whispered, "give my love to the swallow if ever he comes back this way. Now I must go down into the dark forever to be the bride of the gloomy old mole. Goodbye, dear flower. Farewell, bright sun!"

At that moment she heard a flutter of wings. It was her friend the swallow! "Come," he called. "Come with me. I am flying to a land that is warm and full of sunshine."

Thumbelina

So Thumbelina climbed on the swallow's back, tied her belt to one of its strongest feathers, and they were off, flying high into the sunshine, over mountains and forests and blue seas. When night came and the wind blew cold, Thumbelina crept down into the bird's warm feathers.

They came at last to the warm countries. There the sun shone every day, and along the roadsides grew vines from which hung clusters of green and purple grapes. The swallow flew down slowly and set Thumbelina down in a garden fragrant with flowers. Thumbelina clapped her hands with delight to see these beautiful blooms.

As she did so, the petals of the largest flower opened, and standing there she saw a tiny man no larger than herself. How handsome he was! On his head he wore a gold crown, and delicate wings fluttered on his shoulders. Then she saw that every flower held a tiny man or woman, but he was King of them all.

The King of the flowers took off his gold crown and placed it on Thumbelina's head. Then he asked her name and begged her to be his wife. "You will be Queen of all the flowers, and henceforth you will no longer be called Thumbelina, which is an ugly name for one so fair as you. We will call you Queen Maia."

Then everyone brought gifts to their new Queen. The most wonderful gift of all was a pair of bright wings, which they fastened to her shoulders, so that she too could fly from flower to flower.

And that is how Thumbelina became Queen Maia and lived happily ever afterward in the warm and beautiful country far far away.

Cinderella

NEAR the fair city of Paris there once lived a gentleman whose wife had died, leaving him to care for their little daughter, Ella. I cannot bring up the child all by myself, he thought. And so he married again. But what a horrible stepmother to Ella this second wife turned out to be! She was a proud, disagreeable woman, and her two daughters were as disagreeable as their mother. Charlotte and Henriette, for those were their names, were lazy and rude, and Ella had to wait on them besides keeping house. From dawn to dark she mopped the floors and scoured the pots and swept the ashes from the hearth. At night she slept on a hard straw bed in the attic, while her two sisters lay on mattresses of swansdown in gilded bedrooms hung with mirrors and silken draperies.

Ella did not dare to complain to her father, but often she would sit weeping in the chimney corner among the cinders. And so she was called Cinderella. But the ragged clothes and streaks of dirt could not hide her lovely face or her gentle manners.

Several years passed, and then the King's son sent word throughout the kingdom that he was giving a grand ball. Among those invited were Cinderella's two stepsisters.

At once they began to strut before their mirrors, admiring themselves and planning what they should wear. Bright velvet gowns and ruffled petticoats, and yards of the finest lace and ribbons were strewn around their rooms. They kept Cinderella busy day and night running errands to the shops, starching and pressing their petticoats, and sewing the ribbons and lace on their overskirts.

The night of the ball came at last. Cinderella deftly arranged their hair and helped them into their beautiful dresses, but she sighed to think that she must stay at home. Charlotte, the younger, heard her and said, "I'm sure you wish that you too could go to the Prince's ball, Cinderella."

Henriette laughed loudly. "It would certainly make people laugh to see our dirty Cinderwench at the ball!"

Cinderella said nothing. She was as good as she was fair, and she waved and smiled bravely when her two stepsisters climbed into the coach that carried them to the ball.

Cinderella waited until they drove away, and then rushed to her chimney corner and wept and wept. Suddenly she heard a faint sound. She opened her eyes, and there in a blaze of rosy light stood a sweet-faced tiny old lady.

"Don't cry any more, Cinderella," said the lady. "I am your fairy godmother, and since you want to go the ball so very much, you shall go in a manner fit for a Princess. Dry your eyes now and run into the back garden. You will find a pumpkin growing there. Bring it to me, and hurry, for there is no time to be lost!"

Cinderella ran into the dark garden and brought back the pumpkin. Her fairy godmother scooped out the inside, leaving the rind. Then she touched the pumpkin lightly with her wand and at once it turned into the most beautiful golden coach you have ever seen.

"Now fetch me the mousetrap from the pantry," said her godmother. Cinderella did as she was told, and there in the trap sat six mice, which her fairy godmother turned into a team of six prancing white horses.

Cinderella clapped her hands for joy. "Perhaps there is a rat in the rattrap," she said, "and we can make a coachman of him."

Sure enough, when Cinderella brought the rattrap, there sat a huge rat with fine whiskers. The fairy released him and touched him with her wand and he at once turned into a fat coachman with a fine moustache.

Then the godmother said, "You will need footmen. Go into the garden and you will find six lizards near the well. Bring them to me."

Cinderella brought the lizards, and in a wink the magic wand had turned them into six footmen in green and gold livery, who climbed nimbly up to their places on the coach.

Cinderella gazed happily at the coach and horses but then her face fell. "What is the matter? Aren't you pleased with the fine coach which will take you to the Prince's ball?" asked the fairy godmother.

"Yes, it's beautiful! But how can I go in these rags?" asked Cinderella.

"We will soon change all that," said the fairy godmother. She touched Cinderella with her wand and Cinderella turned into a real Princess, from the tips of the snowy ostrich plumes in her powdered hair, to her glass slippers that sparkled like diamonds. Her gown was made of the finest satin and embroidered with jewels and lace.

"Now go and be happy as you deserve," said the godmother. "But I warn you that you must leave the ball before midnight. If you are even one moment late you will find yourself again in rags, and you will have to walk home, for your coach will again be a pumpkin, your horses mice, your coachman a rat, and your footmen lizards."

Cinderella kissed her godmother and promised to remember her warning. When she arrived at the ball, so beautiful did she appear to the Prince that he could not take his eyes from her, and all the ladies and gentlemen of the court praised her beauty and grace, and admired her beautiful gown.

The King himself whispered to the Queen that he had never seen such a lovely maiden. "She has such grace and manners! I'm sure she is a royal Princess," the Queen whispered back.

The Prince danced every dance with Cinderella, and during the feast which followed he never left her side, so enchanted was he by her beauty.

Cinderella, in her joy, shared with her sisters, who were sitting near her, the choicest cakes and fruits on her plate. Of course they did not recognize the lovely stranger.

When she heard the clock strike a quarter to twelve, Cinderella said good night to all the company and hurried away. She reached home safely, and looked for her godmother to thank her, but she had vanished. Soon her stepsisters came in. Cinderella pretended she had been asleep, and greeted them with a yawn. "How late you have stayed!" she said.

"Ah, if you had been at the ball," answered Charlotte, "you too would have stayed late. What music! What delicious food! What a handsome Prince! But that is not all. There came to the ball the most enchanting creature we have ever seen. She is a royal Princess. There can be no doubt of that. How beautiful she was! And her dress! It was made of the finest satin and sparkled with diamonds. To both of us she showed the most marked attention. Everyone noticed it, even the Prince."

"What was the name of this lovely Princess?" asked Cinderella.

"We do not know. Nor does anybody, not even the Prince himself. But they say he would give half his kingdom to see her again."

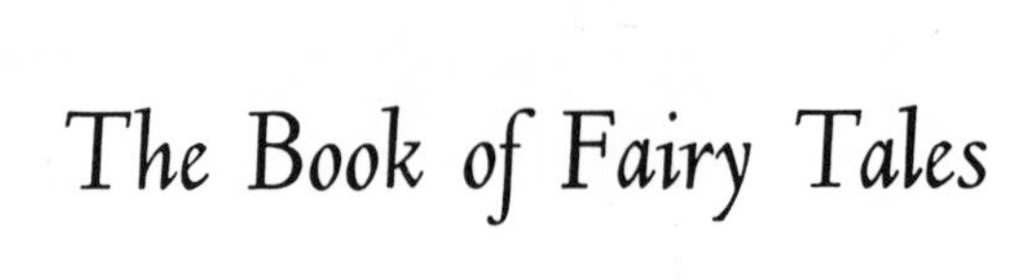

At this, Cinderella's heart leaped for joy, for she had fallen in love with the handsome Prince. "She must have been beautiful," she said to her sisters. "How fortunate you both were to see her! Perhaps I could borrow your old yellow gown, Henriette, and go to see her for myself."

Her stepsister laughed scornfully. "What? Do you really think that a Cinderwench like you would be admitted to the Prince's ball? A pretty picture you would be! Besides, I would never lend you my yellow gown, or any other clothes, until I have quite worn them out."

Cinderella smiled to herself. She had been jesting, for she certainly did not want to appear at the ball in Henriette's old yellow gown.

The following night the two stepsisters again went to the ball, and again Cinderella helped them dress and watched them drive away, wondering if she would be able to follow them to the ball later on.

No sooner had the coach departed than the fairy godmother appeared. As on the evening before, she changed the pumpkin to a gilded coach, the mice to horses, the rat to a handsome coachman, the lizards to footmen, and Cinderella's rags to a gown even more magnificent than the one she had worn before. And again she warned her about the midnight hour. Cinderella promised not to forget.

This time the Prince again danced every dance with her. He told her over and over again how beautiful she was and begged her to tell him her name. She refused to do this. But she was enjoying herself so much that she did not remember her godmother's warning until she heard the palace clock begin to strike twelve.

In alarm she hastily left the astonished prince, and ran through the long halls of the palace and out into the night. As she ran down the steps, one of her glass slippers came off and was left behind. The Prince, in trying to

overtake her, came upon the little glass slipper and picked it up most carefully. He asked the guards whether they had seen a lovely Princess leaving the palace, but they only shook their heads. No one had passed, they said, but a young girl dressed in rags.

Cinderella, very tired and out of breath, reached home with the other glass slipper hidden in her pocket. When the two stepsisters returned from the ball, she asked them if the Princess had been there.

Yes, they replied, she had been there and the Prince had danced only with her. But as the clock struck twelve she had left suddenly, and in such haste that one of her dainty glass slippers had fallen off onto the marble steps. The Prince, they said, had found the slipper and had spent some time looking for its owner and questioning the guards and gatekeeper, but the lovely stranger had vanished.

Cinderella wished that she might see the Prince again, but she knew that was impossible without her fairy godmother, who was probably angry with her for not heeding her warning.

A few days later it was proclaimed that the Prince would marry the girl upon whose foot the glass slipper fitted perfectly. What a stir there was in the land! First the Princesses, then the Duchesses and ladies of the Court, and then the ladies of wealth and position each tried to force her foot into the dainty slipper. But it was too tiny for all of them.

Finally, the messengers knocked at the door of Cinderella's house. The two stepsisters both tried to squeeze their feet into the tiny slipper, but it was far too small for them. Cinderella, who was standing beside them, said, "May I try? Perhaps it would fit me."

The sisters shouted with laughter. But the royal messenger had noticed Cinderella's beauty, and courteously asked her to sit down while he tried the slipper on her foot. It fitted her as though made of wax! The sisters were too astonished to speak, but even more surprised were they when Cinderella took from her pocket the matching slipper and slipped it easily on her other tiny foot.

Suddenly the fairy godmother stood in their midst. She waved her wand and immediately Cinderella became the enchanting Princess who had been at the ball, dressed even more beautifully than before. And now the two stepsisters fell on their knees, begging her forgiveness for their meanness and cruelty to her. Cinderella bade them rise and embraced them both, saying she forgave them gladly, and begging them to love her always.

When the Prince saw her he fell more in love with her than ever. So they were married and lived happily ever after.

Jack and the Beanstalk

NOT FAR from London there once lived a widow and her son, Jack. They were so poor that often they didn't have enough to eat, and as Jack was a lazy boy who never liked to work, matters grew worse and worse for his poor mother.

Then a day came when they had to sell their cow. With tears in her eyes the poor woman told Jack to take the cow to market and get the best price he could for it.

So Jack, leading the cow, set off. He had not gone far when he met a man who asked him, "Are you taking your cow to market, Jack?"

"Yes," answered Jack, wondering how the stranger knew his name.

"I will buy the cow from you," said the man. "I have some magic beans here that I will give you in exchange for the cow."

Jack couldn't resist the wonderful-looking beans that the man showed him, and gladly gave the cow to the man in exchange.

When his mother learned what he had done, she burst into tears and threw the beans out of the window.

As for Jack, he crept off to bed without his supper, feeling very much ashamed of himself, and hungry as well.

But the next morning when he looked from his window he saw a wonderful sight. The beans had taken root in the garden overnight, and the great stalks twined together, forming an enormous ladder leading up, up into the sky as far as he could see.

Forgetting everything else, Jack climbed from his window into the beanstalk. He climbed and he climbed, and at the very top he found himself in a strange and silent country.

He was tired and hungry, and looking about he was glad to see a great castle not far away. He walked to the castle and knocked at the door.

A tall woman opened it, and said, "What do you want?"

"Can you give me some bread and a place to spend the night?" Jack asked. "I am tired and hungry."

The woman shook her head. "If you weren't a stranger here you would know that my husband is a giant ogre, who likes nothing better than to eat human flesh. Please go away. Your life will be in great danger if you stay."

But Jack coaxed her to let him stay, even though the thought of the giant frightened him. The woman, who had a kind heart, led him into the kitchen, and gave him some hot soup and bread.

Scarcely had Jack begun to eat the hot soup when there came a frightful banging on the outside door. "Quick! Hide in the oven!" whispered the woman as she ran to let in her husband. The moment the giant entered the house he roared:

Fee Fi Fo Fum!
I smell the blood
of an Englishman!
Be he alive or be he dead
I'll grind his bones to make my bread!

But his wife said, "It is only some bones the ravens have dropped down the chimney that you smell."

The giant grumbled, and sat down by the fireside to eat his supper. Jack watched him through a crack in the oven.

The giant ate steadily for a long time, but at last he wiped his mouth on a corner of the tablecloth and shouted, "Wife, fetch me my bags of gold!" His wife went to a huge cupboard and got down three bags, so heavy she could scarcely carry them, and set them on the table beside the giant. He dumped the shining coins onto the tablecloth, and Jack's eyes grew round. He had never seen so much money before in his life.

The giant scooped them into a pile and spent a long time counting them into another pile. Then he began to nod. He had not finished putting his treasure back into the bags before he fell fast asleep. Jack crept stealthily out of the oven and was just reaching for a bag of gold when to his horror, a little dog ran out and began to bark at him. The giant stirred and muttered, but he did not wake up, and the dog went back to his place under the chair by the fire.

Quickly Jack seized one of the bags and ran out of the house, down the highway, and so to the top of the beanstalk and home. His mother had worried because Jack had been gone a day and a night, but when she saw the bag of gold he had brought her she was overjoyed, and called him the best son in the world. Jack was very happy to hear this, you may be sure, and for a long time he and his mother lived very well on all the fine things they could buy with the money.

There came a day, however, when only a few coins were left, and Jack resolved to climb the beanstalk once again and visit the giant's castle. This time he waited outside the castle until the bakery man came to deliver twenty loaves of bread the size of mill wheels at the kitchen door. Then Jack crept in while the door was open and hid in a huge copper pot.

Soon the giant came home for dinner. As soon as he entered the house he looked about him and roared:

Fee Fi Fo Fum,
I smell the blood
of an Englishman!

"Nonsense, dear," said his wife. "It is the remains of a squirrel that the ravens have dropped down the chimney." The giant grumbled louder this time, but he sat down to a whole roast pig and a goblet of wine the size of a goldfish bowl.

After dinner the giant called for his little hen. The woman fetched it and set the pretty golden hen on the table.

Every time the giant said,

Little hen, pretty hen,
Lay me an egg,

the little hen clucked and sang, and laid an egg of solid gold.

Jack opened his eyes at this, you may be sure, and decided he must and would have that hen for himself. Soon the giant began to nod, and before long fell asleep, snoring horribly. Then, being careful not to make any noise, Jack crept out of the copper pot, seized the hen, and ran off with her.

He found his way back to the beanstalk much more quickly than he had come. He climbed down and reached the house just at dusk. His mother had worried for fear Jack had fallen into the hands of the giant. She was overjoyed to see him and the pretty hen he had brought her.

Jack and the Beanstalk

With the little hen laying golden eggs every day Jack and his mother were soon well off again, and for a few months this suited Jack very well. But soon he became restless for adventure, and so he decided to climb the beanstalk one more time.

As before, the tall woman opened the door. She did not recognize Jack in the fine new clothes he had been able to buy with the golden eggs.

She told him of another boy who had come some time earlier, asking for food and lodging. She had taken pity on him and he had rewarded her kindness by stealing one of her husband's treasures. Since then her husband had been more of an ogre than ever, and she had sworn never to give shelter or food to another stranger. However, Jack pleaded with her, and so she took him in. She gave him supper and hid him in the wood box.

This evening the giant stamped into the house, roaring so loudly the pots rattled on the stove:

Fee Fi Fo Fum,
I smell the blood
of an Englishman!

"What foolishness! Do you think I would let in another boy to steal from us?" asked his wife. "It is nothing but a young rabbit the ravens have dropped down the chimney."

The giant grumbled but he sat down to a bowl the size of a wash tub filled with stew, and began to eat noisily.

After supper he called for his harp.

Jack lifted the lid of the wood box to see the most beautiful harp imaginable standing on the table. The giant had only to say, "Play!" and exquisite music came from the instrument.

Here was a treasure Jack wanted much more than the magic hen. "I will surely steal that wonderful harp, come what will," said Jack to himself.

In a little while the lovely music had lulled the giant to sleep. Jack waited until he heard the giant snoring loudly. Then he got out of the wood box and stole over to the table.

As he was reaching for the harp it began to cry, "Master! Master!" But Jack seized it and ran to the heavy door. He just managed to pull it open before the giant woke up with a mighty roar, and started after him.

Jack had never been so terrified or run so fast in his life. Yet the giant, with his huge steps, soon overcame the distance between them. Jack could feel the giant's breath, like a hot wind, on his back, and he reached the beanstalk only just in time.

With the giant right behind him, Jack clambered down more quickly than I would like to think, with the beanstalk swaying and creaking with the weight of the pursuing giant.

Once on the ground, Jack shouted for a hatchet, and his mother came flying out of the house with one in her hand. Quickly, and with all his might, Jack began hacking at the great beanstalk until it fell with a mighty crash to the earth, killing the giant instantly.

Jack asked his mother to forgive him for all the trouble he had caused her and promised never to go adventuring again. He kept his word and they lived happily and well for the rest of their lives.

Rumpelstiltskin

THERE was once a miller who had a pretty daughter One day he had business at Court, and thinking to make himself important in the eyes of the King, he boasted, "I have a daughter who is so clever she can spin gold out of straw."

"That is very hard to believe," answered the King, "but if your daughter can really do what you say, send her to the castle in the morning and we shall see how clever she is."

So in the morning the girl came to the castle and the King led her to a room full of straw. Pointing to a spinning wheel in one corner, he said, "There is your work awaiting you. If between tonight and tomorrow's dawn you have not spun this straw into gold you must die." With this the King left her, locking the door behind him.

The miller's daughter sat down at the spinning wheel and began to cry, for although she could spin with skill, she had no idea how to spin gold from straw. Suddenly the door sprang open and an old dwarf stepped into the room. "Good evening," said he. "Why are you weeping?"

"Alas!" cried the girl, "I must spin this straw into gold before dawn or I will die, and I don't know how to do it."

"What will you give me if I do it for you?" asked the dwarf.

"I will give you my necklace." said the girl.

"Very well," said the dwarf. He put the necklace in his pocket. Then he sat at the spinning wheel, and whir, whir, he spun the straw into gold.

When the King came at dawn he was astonished to see the gold, for he thought he had set the girl an impossible task. Of course, he was very pleased, but he was also a greedy man. So he led the miller's daughter to a larger room filled with straw and ordered her to spin it into gold or die when morning came. At her wits' end the poor girl again fell to weeping. As before, the dwarf appeared, offering to help if she would give him something in exchange.

"I will give you my ring," said the miller's daughter.

The dwarf took the ring, sat down at the spinning wheel, and whir, whir, went the wheel. By dawn all the straw was spun into gold. The King was overjoyed, but he wanted still more gold. This time he led the miller's daughter into an even larger room filled with straw and said, "All this you must spin into gold before tomorrow morning or you will die, but if you succeed you shall become Queen."

For the third time the frightened girl sat hopelessly weeping and for the third time the dwarf came, asking what she would give him if he spun the straw into gold.

"I have nothing more to give," she answered.

"Then promise me your first child if you become Queen."

I *may* become Queen but who knows? thought the girl, so she promised him her first child, and whir, whir, he spun the straw into gold.

In the morning, when the King saw the room piled high with gold, he was so delighted that he and the miller's daughter were married at once, with great rejoicing in the kingdom.

A year later a child was born to the young Queen. She was very happy, and forgot all about her promise to the dwarf. Then one day when she was alone with the baby the door opened and there stood the dwarf.

"I have come for the child you promised to me," he said.

The Queen begged him not to be so cruel and said she would give him half the wealth of the kingdom if he would just let her keep the child. But the dwarf shook his head. "No," he said. "Wealth means nothing to me. I want a living creature of my own. I want the child."

However, the Queen wept so piteously that at last he was sorry for her. "Three days you may have to discover my name. If you do, you may keep the child."

All through the night the Queen lay awake trying to think of a likely name, and meanwhile she had messengers sent out all over the country to inquire for unusual names. When the dwarf came the next day, she began with names like Melchior, Obed, Arabacus and others, but to each the dwarf shook his head and said, "No, that is not my name."

The second day the Queen went all about the countryside, asking for names of people living there, and when the dwarf came that evening she asked him, "Would your name by chance be Gooseneck, Spindleshanks, or Spiderlegs?"

But he answered, "No, my name is none of these."

Rumpelstiltskin

The Queen was in despair. But at noon on the third day, one of her messengers came to her and said, "Last evening when the wind blew cold I was riding through a wood. There I came upon a hut. In front of it a fire of faggots was burning and around it danced a little man with a black cat. As he danced he sang:

Today I bake; tomorrow I brew beer.
The next day I bring the Queen's child here.
Lucky it is not a soul doth know
My name is Rumpelstiltskin, O.

With what thankfulness the Queen heard that name! When evening came the dwarf appeared. "Now, Your Majesty, what is my name?"

She answered, "Is your name John?"

"No," shouted the dwarf.

"Is it Jason?"

"No, neither is it Jason, Your Majesty."

"By chance, then, is it Rumpelstiltskin?" she asked.

"A witch has told you that!" he screamed, and in his rage he stamped his foot so deeply into the ground that he sank in up to his waist. Then, in a fury, he seized his other leg with both hands and so split himself in two, and that was the end of the old dwarf.

Mr. Samson Cat

ONCE upon a time a cat met a fox in a shady wood.

"Good day, fox. What is your name?" he asked.

"I am called the Widow Fox," she answered. "What is your name?"

"I am Mr. Samson Cat," said he. "I should very much like to live in this wood."

"You may come and live in my house," said Widow Fox. So she and the cat set up housekeeping.

Now one day Mr. Samson Cat was out looking for catnip when a careless rabbit jumped on him by mistake.

"MEOW, psssst," said Mr. Samson Cat, which so terrified the rabbit that he ran until he could run no further. He threw himself down, panting.

Along came a wolf. "Well, Big Eyes, why are you in such a flurry?"

"Flurry indeed!" said the rabbit. "I've only just escaped with my life. A frightful beast at Widow Fox's leaped upon me as I was walking by. If I hadn't been so nimble I would have been eaten alive."

"I must have a look at this animal," said the wolf, and trotted off to Widow Fox's house.

Now Widow Fox and Mr. Samson Cat had dragged a bit of deer meat into their house, and were eating it when the wolf knocked at the door.

T. Tudor

"Good afternoon, Widow Fox. May I ask who it is you have staying with you in your house?" said the wolf.

"Oh, that's the mighty Mr. Samson Cat, eating a deer he killed in a fight. You'd better go away before he eats you, too."

The wolf heard Mr. Samson Cat crying, "Mee-ow, mee-ow," and thought he was saying, "Not enough, not enough." Well this *is* a dreadful animal, thought the wolf, and ran away.

As he was running, he met a pig. "Have you heard the news?" he panted. "Widow Fox has got the mighty Mr. Samson Cat living with her. He eats four deer a day, and then says he hasn't had enough. This forest is no longer safe for any of us."

Just then a bear came along. The pig said to him, "Did you hear that Widow Fox has the mighty Mr. Samson Cat living with her? He eats ten deer a day, and then says he hasn't had enough!"

"How dreadful!" said the bear. "What does this animal look like?"

But nobody knew. "We must go and have a peep at Mr. Samson Cat," said the wolf. So they went to Widow Fox's house and knocked at the door.

"We have heard about your Mr. Samson Cat and would like to have a look at him. Can you arrange this so that he doesn't eat us up?"

Widow Fox thought a bit and said, "Yes, I think so. You must bake a lot of pies and tomorrow invite us to come and eat them. And then *perhaps* the mighty Mr. Samson Cat won't do you any harm."

So the bear and the wolf and the pig worked all the next morning baking pies and tidying up.

After a while the bear said, "Ahem, I believe I shall climb to the top of this tree so that I can see the guests when they arrive." He climbed up the tree and hid among the branches, trembling with fright.

Mr. Samson Cat

The wolf yawned. "I've been making pies all day and I'm tired," he said. "I think I'll rest a bit under this log." He crawled under the log and lay down there, wishing he had not been so curious about Mr. Samson Cat.

The pig said, "I'm tired and hot from cleaning up. I'll just go and sit in the shade for a bit." He hid himself in the underbrush.

Soon Widow Fox and Mr. Samson Cat came to the clearing. There were the pies, but the wolf, the pig and the bear were nowhere to be seen.

"We'll have to eat without our hosts," said Widow Fox. So she and Mr. Samson Cat fell to, gobbling up the pies in no time at all.

Suddenly Mr. Samson Cat heard a rustling in the underbrush. It was really the pig's tail, twitching with fright. "That must be a mouse," said Mr. Samson Cat, and pounced upon the horrified pig, who was so frightened he dashed headlong into a stump. Mr. Samson Cat, who was as frightened as the pig, jumped into the very tree in which the bear was hiding. The bear was so terrified that he lost his hold and fell right on top of the log under which the wolf lay hidden. The wolf thought, my end has come, and lost no time in making himself scarce.

That evening the wolf, the pig and the bear met and told each other their experiences. The pig said, "Did you see him dash my head against a stump?" The bear said, "That was nothing. He tore up the tree I was in, by the roots. No wonder I couldn't hold on!"

And the wolf said, "None of you had such a narrow escape as I did. He brought that big oak tree right down on the log where I was resting."

"Yes, indeed," said the bear and wolf and the pig. "This forest is no longer safe for the likes of us, with an animal like Mr. Samson Cat around."

Sleeping Beauty

IN A FAR country long, long ago there lived a King and Queen who lacked but one thing to make them perfectly happy: a child. One day, while the Queen was bathing, a frog hopped along the bank and spoke to her in this fashion, "Your wish to have a child shall be granted. Within a year you shall have a beautiful little daughter."

True enough, the Queen had a little girl who was so fair, so lovely, that the King was beside himself with joy. He sent out invitations for a great feast. Everyone was invited, friends, relations, acquaintances, and even the fairies, for the King and Queen wanted their kind favor for the child. Now there were thirteen fairies in the kingdom, and alas, but twelve gold plates in the palace, so one fairy had to stay at home.

She was an evil fairy and was angered because she was not invited to the feast. While the other fairies were giving the little Princess their magic gifts of virtue, beauty, kindness and compassion, the wicked fairy suddenly appeared before the company.

Sleeping Beauty

Without greeting anyone, she went straight to the cradle of the little Princess, and shaking her stick above the innocent child's head, she cried, "When the Princess is fifteen years old she will prick herself with a spindle and shall die!" Then she vanished with a clap of thunder.

Everyone was horrified. The twelfth fairy had fortunately still her gift to bestow. She now came forward, and quieting the distressed parents and guests, she said, "I cannot prevent this evil spell but I can soften it. Instead of dying, the Princess shall fall into a deep sleep, lasting a hundred years."

So great was the King's fear for his little daughter, however, that he had every spindle in his kingdom destroyed, and spinning became a lost art.

As time passed and the little Princess grew older, the promises of the fairies came true. She was gentle and beautiful and modest and kind, and everyone loved her.

It so happened that on her fifteenth birthday the King and Queen went to a nearby kingdom on a matter of business, and the Princess was left alone in the palace. For long hours she amused herself, but growing weary of her embroidery and music, she started to wander through the many rooms and passageways of the castle.

She was surprised to discover a part of the castle she had never seen before, an old tower reached by a winding stair. She climbed up, and at the top came upon a small room in which sat an old old woman, spinning. The Princess was fascinated by the whirling spindle, and after greeting the old woman she asked if she might try to spin, too. No sooner had she taken the spindle into her hand than she pricked herself, and instantly fell into a deep sleep.

When the King and Queen came home and entered the castle, they too were overcome with sleep, as were the knights and ladies, the servants and

the kitchen maids. The fire on the hearth died down, the doves in the eaves put their heads under their wings, and the horses in the stables stood sleeping in their stalls. The hounds and the falcons, the cats and the birds, and even the little gray mice, all slept the deep sleep of enchantment.

A hedge of brier roses grew up around the castle, climbing higher and higher every year until the whole castle was hidden by them.

A legend about the Sleeping Beauty in the castle spread across the land, and Princes came to try and force their way through the thorny hedge. Too late they found it could not be done and died miserably in the grasp of the thorns.

T. Tudor

Many years passed. Then, one day, a handsome Prince came from a far country in search of adventure. A peasant told him the story of the castle behind the hedge of thorns and of the lovely sleeping Princess. The old peasant had the story from his own grandfather, of how the Princess had been bewitched by an evil fairy a hundred years ago, and of how she and everyone in the castle had been asleep ever since.

"I must and shall see this lovely Princess," declared the Prince, and though the old peasant tried to dissuade him, the Prince would not listen. His longing to see the Sleeping Beauty was far greater than his fear of the thorny hedge, so he set out in high spirits.

He was surprised, upon coming to the castle, to see the hedge burst into bloom, and when he approached, the thorny branches opened for him. On this very day the hundred years' enchantment had come to an end!

The Prince made his way into the castle through a silence so profound that only the beating of his heart and the echo of his footsteps disturbed it. He came to the old tower and climbed the winding stairs to the little room where lay the Sleeping Beauty.

The Prince looked down at the lovely Princess a long time, for he had never seen anyone so beautiful. Then he stooped and kissed her, whereupon she opened her eyes and smiled at him, and the evil spell was at an end.

The King and Queen awakened, as did the knights and ladies. The horses whinnied from the stables, the dogs barked, and the falcons stretched their beautiful wings. The fire crackled brightly on the hearth, and the cooks and kitchen maids went back to their work.

The wedding of the Prince and the Princess was celebrated with a great feast, and they lived happily ever afterwards.

The Emperor's New Clothes

LONG, LONG AGO there was an Emperor who was more interested in clothes than anything else in the world. He had a special outfit for every day of the week, and every hour of the day.

One day two rogues came to town, pretending they were expert weavers and tailors. The two men set up a loom and spread the news that they wove the finest of cloth, in the most beautiful designs and colors. But, said they, only a really wise man could see it, for to stupid, dull or foolish people it was completely invisible.

The Emperor said he must have a suit of this marvelous cloth. So he immediately sent for these men and ordered them to make him a royal costume. He gave them a bag of gold and told them to spare no expense.

The two rogues stuffed their purses and made a great show of working on the empty looms at all hours of the day and night. Two weeks went by, then the Emperor, who could hardly wait to try on his wonderful new clothes, sent his trusted minister to see how the work was going.

When the minister arrived at the shop he saw the two rogues hard at work, going through all the motions of weaving. He could see no cloth, but the two men described the lovely colors and delicate designs in such glowing words that the minister thought, I must be the greatest fool in the kingdom, for I can see nothing! Yet if I tell the Emperor that the looms are bare, he will think I am stupid and discharge me. I had better repeat to him the words of the weavers. So he went back to the Emperor and praised the rich color and delicate patterns.

A week later, when the cloth was still not finished, the Emperor sent another trusted official to examine the weavers' work. The official could see nothing on the loom, either, because of course there was nothing there to see. But he did not want to be thought a fool, so he, too, praised the cloth, telling the Emperor that its gorgeous design would be sure to dazzle all who beheld it.

The Emperor was growing so very impatient that he decided to see for himself. With a party of courtiers he arrived at the shop of the two rogues who were weaving at the empty loom.

"Did Your Majesty ever behold such gorgeous material?" asked the one. "Just feel the quality!" said the other. Bewildered, the Emperor looked at his courtiers, but they were all smiling, exclaiming, "Exquisite!" "Perfect!" and "Magnificent!" The Emperor said to himself, "No one must know how stupid I am." And he, too, began to praise the cloth that wasn't there.

Soon the great Procession of the Year was to take place, and the two rogues promised the Emperor that his new suit would be ready for the occasion. Each of the men was given a knight's medal to hang in his button-hole and with it the title of "Gentleman in Weaving."

T. Tudor

The night before the Procession, the two rogues worked late into the night making the royal costume. They lit all the candles in the shop so that everyone could see they were hard at work. They snipped the empty air with scissors, they sewed with threadless needles, and at last they pulled out the long bastings, stood up, and shook out the beautiful clothes that were not there.

In the morning the Emperor came to try on the suit. He stood straight and still while he let them take away his clothes and put on the imaginary new ones. "Light as a spider's web," said the one, going through the motions of slipping on the coat. "What superb color!" said the other, throwing the invisible mantle over the Emperor's shoulder. And the attending courtiers echoed, "Superb! Superb!"

So the Emperor walked proudly under the royal canopy in the Procession. He was sure that his new clothes made him look magnificent, although he could not see them.

He bowed graciously to the left and right, as the people cried, "How splendid are the Emperor's new clothes! How beautifully they fit! Such color, such rare and costly cloth!"

Then all at once a little child cried, "But he hasn't got anything on!" And though his mother hushed him quickly, the Emperor had heard. Perhaps the child was right! The thought made his flesh creep but he knew that being the Emperor, he must lead the Procession through to the end. So he squared his shoulders and held his head high while the lords in waiting followed, bearing the train that wasn't there at all!

Rapunzel

IN A VILLAGE near a forest in Germany there once lived a woodcarver and his wife. They had long wished for a child and finally they knew that their wish would come true.

Now the wife liked to sit and look from her upstairs window into the garden next door. It belonged to a witch, and all sorts of wonderful flowers and vegetables grew there. One day the wife noticed a patch of salad greens. These salad greens are called rapunzel in Germany. They looked so crisp and delicious that the woman's mouth watered for them. The more she gazed on the shining green leaves the more her longing for them increased until she grew sick and weak, and her husband feared she would die if she could not have some of the witch's rapunzel. So one evening he climbed over the garden wall to get some for her.

But no sooner had he begun to gather the rapunzel than the old witch appeared before him. "What are you doing here in my garden, thief?" she demanded, shaking her stick at him.

"Have pity, good witch. My wife is ill with longing for your beautiful rapunzel, and if she does not eat some she will die."

"So!" answered the witch. "In that case, you may take as much as you like. But for this favor I demand a promise in return. You must give me your child when she is born. I will not harm her, but have her I will."

The terrified husband made the dreadful promise and took the rapunzel to his wife. She lay weak and deathly pale, but as soon as she had eaten a salad of the rapunzel greens she became rosy and well again.

A few months later a little girl was born, and within the hour the witch appeared, lifted the infant from its cradle and carried it away in spite of the parents' pleading. She named the child Rapunzel, for the plant that had delivered the child into her hands.

Every year Rapunzel grew more beautiful. Her hair grew so long that it hung in a heavy braid to the floor, and every year it grew longer. She sang so sweetly that the birds stopped singing to listen.

When Rapunzel was twelve the witch took her deep in the forest, to a high tower that had neither door nor staircase, but only a window, up under the roof. When the witch wanted to visit Rapunzel she would stand beneath the window and call:

Rapunzel, Rapunzel,
Let down your golden hair.

Then Rapunzel would fasten her hair around a hook by the window, and let down the long braid, and the witch would climb up.

Rapunzel spent three lonely years in the tower. The forest birds were her only friends.

Rapunzel

One summer's day a Prince was riding through the forest and heard Rapunzel singing. Never had he heard such an enchanting voice. He rode close to the tower from whence the singing seemed to come, but he could find no entrance, so he decided to hide and wait to see what happened. Soon along came the witch. She went up to the tower and called:

Rapunzel, Rapunzel,
Let down your golden hair.

Rapunzel let her hair down from the window, and the witch climbed up.

If that is the only way to reach the lovely singer, thought the Prince, I will try it myself. So when the witch had gone away the Prince called:

Rapunzel, Rapunzel,
Let down your golden hair.

In a moment the long golden braid came tumbling down and the Prince climbed up. Rapunzel was startled to see a stranger, but the Prince spoke gently to her. "I have heard your sweet singing, and now that I have seen how beautiful you are I cannot live without you. Come with me. I will take you to my kingdom and make you my wife."

Rapunzel clasped her hand in his, but her eyes filled with tears. "Alas," she said. "There is no way out of this tower for me, unless you will return and bring a skein of silk each time. Then I can weave a ladder and we can escape. But be very sure to come only in the evening, for the witch visits me in the daytime."

The Prince promised that he would return every evening until the ladder was finished. Then he rode away.

T. Tudor

Rapunzel

So the witch came each day, and each evening the Prince came, bringing a skein of silk. The witch knew nothing about it until one day, when the ladder was almost finished, Rapunzel said dreamily to her, "Why is it you are so much heavier to draw up than the young Prince?"

"Wicked child!" shrieked the witch. "You have deceived me! I will put you where your Prince will never find you." She seized Rapunzel's hair, and taking a pair of scissors from her pocket, she cut off the thick braid. Then she banished Rapunzel to a wilderness far beyond the forest.

That evening the witch fastened Rapunzel's golden braid to the hook by the window, and when she heard the Prince call:

Rapunzel, Rapunzel,
Let down your golden hair

she dropped the long braid out the window. The Prince climbed up, but there instead of his beautiful Rapunzel stood the ugly witch.

"So!" she shrieked. "You have come for your little dove. Well, the bird has flown, and you will never see her again."

The Prince was so distracted that he leaped out of the high window. The thorn trees caught him and saved his life, but the sharp thorns scratched his eyes and he could no longer see.

The poor Prince wandered for two years until one day he came to the place where Rapunzel was. She instantly recognized her Prince even though he was blind and in rags. Her tears of pity fell upon his blinded eyes and his sight was restored. Then the Prince took her to his kingdom and they lived happily ever after.

The Flying Trunk

LONG, LONG AGO a wealthy merchant left a fortune to his son. The son spent it freely and lived a merry life. He went to a fancy ball every night. He ate the best food, and wore the most costly clothes, and entertained his friends like a king. So the money went, until nothing was left but a few cents, and a pair of slippers and a dressing gown. Nobody noticed him any more. But one of his friends sent him an old trunk with a note saying, "Pack up." There was nothing to pack, so he got into the trunk himself.

It was a remarkable trunk, for the minute you pressed the lock it flew up in the air. Whizz! It flew up through the chimney, and high above the clouds—with the merchant's son inside. On and on went the trunk, to the far land of Turkey, where it landed. The young man hid the trunk in a wood and went into the town. His dressing gown and slippers were not noticed, for the people there wore robes and slippers all day long. He met a man and asked, "What is that great palace close by the town, with the windows set high above the roof?"

"The King's daughter lives there," the man said. "Nobody is allowed to visit her except in the presence of the King and Queen."

"Thank you," said the merchant's son. He went back for his trunk and flew to the palace roof and crept in the window to the Princess.

She was lying on a sofa, asleep. She soon awoke and was terribly startled, until the merchant's son told her he was a Turkish god who had come down to her from the sky. That pleased her very much. So they sat side by side, and he told her some wonderful stories. Then he proposed to the Princess and she at once said, "Yes."

"Come here on Saturday," she said. "The King and Queen will be here for tea. They will be very proud that I am marrying a Turkish god. But be sure you have a really beautiful story ready, for my parents are particularly fond of stories. My mother likes them to be instructive and my father likes them to be funny."

"Yes, I shall bring no wedding gift but a story," said the merchant's son. The Princess gave him a sword set with gold coins, and they parted. The merchant's son flew back to the wood. Then taking his sword he walked into the city and sold it, and bought himself a fine new dressing gown and slippers. When Saturday came he flew to the palace roof. The King and Queen and all the Court were waiting to greet him.

"Will you tell us a story?" asked the Queen, "one that has a deep meaning and is instructive?"

"But a story I can laugh at," added the King.

So the merchant's son told a story—one that was both instructive and funny, which was not easy to do. The King and Queen were so delighted that the King said, "You may have our daughter's hand in marriage, and we will prepare for the wedding immediately."

The Flying Trunk

On the evening before the wedding, the merchant's son bought some rockets and all kinds of fireworks. He put them in his trunk and flew up in the air, and lighted them. Whizz! How they popped and flashed! Never before had the people seen such sights in the heavens. They could see now that it really was the Turkish god who was to marry the Princess.

As soon as the merchant's son had landed his trunk in the wood he went into town to hear what people were saying about the fireworks. And what stories the people told! "I saw the Turkish god himself," said one. "He had eyes like stars and a beard like foaming water." "He was flying in a mantle of fire," said another, "and angels peered from the folds of it."

The merchant's son was delighted. He went back to his trunk—but where was it? A spark from the fireworks had remained inside the trunk and it was burned to ashes. Never again could he fly up to the Princess on the roof, never again pretend to be a Turkish god. That very night he went sadly away and has wandered about the world ever since.

Puss in Boots

IN A LITTLE village in France, there was once a miller who left to his three sons his mill, his donkey, and his cat. The eldest received the mill and the second son inherited the donkey, but the youngest son had only the cat.

"My two brothers can live very well by sharing their mill and their donkey," said the youngest son, "but what can I do with a cat? He is not even good to eat."

The cat heard all this, and said to him, "Do not fret, my master. Just give me a bag for catching game, and a pair of boots, and you will see that I am worth more to you than you think."

Though the miller's son did not pay much attention to what the cat said, he had seen him play clever tricks in catching rats and mice, and decided to give him a pair of stout boots and a game bag. Perhaps Puss could help him after all. So, in his new boots and with the bag about his neck, Puss in Boots went into a briar patch where he knew some rabbits lived. He put some bran into the bag and lay down beside it, pretending to be dead.

Soon a fat young rabbit jumped into the bag. Puss in Boots quickly drew the strings tight and killed the rabbit, which he immediately carried to the palace and presented to His Majesty, the King.

"I have brought, Sire," he said, "a rabbit which my noble lord, the Marquis of Carabas, has commanded me to present to Your Majesty with his compliments."

"Tell your master," said the King, "that I am well pleased."

Then Puss in Boots hid himself in the cornfields, with his bag. A brace of partridges ran into it, he drew the strings and snared them. These, too, he presented to the King, who gave him a purse of gold and thanked him.

For several months Puss in Boots carried various kinds of game to His Majesty, which he presented in the name of his master. One day while at the King's palace, he heard that the King and his beautiful daughter would be driving near the river that afternoon. So he said to his master, "If you will do as I say, you will make your fortune. Go to the river and bathe at the spot where the river runs closest to the road, and leave the rest to me."

The "Marquis of Carabas," as Puss in Boots called the miller's son, thought the idea was foolish. "But," he said to himself, "Puss in Boots has brought me a purse of gold from the King. I will follow his advice."

He was bathing in the river as the King's coach came by. Immediately Puss in Boots ran into the road and shouted, "Help! Help! My lord the Marquis of Carabas is drowning!"

The King lowered the window of the coach and saw his friend Puss in Boots, who often supplied him with game. He ordered his guards to assist the drowning "Marquis."

While they were helping the miller's son out of the river, Puss in Boots approached the coach and told the King that some ruffians had stolen his master's clothes. He had shouted, "Stop, thief!" several times, he said, but he was powerless to stop them. (The cunning Puss in Boots had really hidden his master's clothes under a stone!) The King sent his servants for one of his finest suits to clothe the "Marquis of Carabas."

In his new clothes, the handsome miller's son really looked like a marquis. The King's daughter fell deeply in love with him, and the King invited him to enter the coach to share their outing.

Delighted that his plan was succeeding, Puss in Boots ran on ahead. When he came to some farmers mowing hay in a meadow, he said to them, "Good people, if you do not tell the King when he passes by that this meadow belongs to the Marquis of Carabas, you shall lose your lives."

Soon His Majesty drove up to the farmers and asked them who owned the meadow they were mowing. The frightened farmers shouted in a chorus, "To the great Marquis of Carabas!"

"A fine property you have here," the King complimented the Marquis.

Puss in Boots hurried on, and seeing some reapers in a cornfield he warned them with these words: "Good people, if you do not say that this corn belongs to the Marquis of Carabas, you shall be cut into mincemeat."

A few minutes later the King, in passing, was told by the frightened reapers that all the fine corn belonged to the Marquis of Carabas. So as Puss in Boots sped on ahead, the King was ever more astonished at the vast estates of the Marquis of Carabas.

Puss in Boots went on until he reached the house of the rich ogre, who really owned the land through which they had been passing. "Tell me," he said to the ogre, "is it true that you can change yourself into any beast you care to—a lion perhaps?"

"Yes, indeed. Look!" answered the ogre proudly. And behold a great lion faced the frightened Puss in Boots, who leaped up on the roof. In his heavy boots he barely escaped the teeth of the ferocious lion. But when the lion had turned back into an ogre, Puss in Boots came down and said flatteringly, "And is it true that you can also make yourself into a small animal like say—a mouse?"

"Simple, indeed," boasted the ogre. He at once transformed himself into a mouse, whereupon Puss in Boots pounced on him and ate him up!

Just then, the King approached in his coach and Puss in Boots ran out, shouting, "Welcome to the castle of my lord the Marquis of Carabas!"

The King never dreamed that there was a castle like this anywhere in his kingdom. It was almost as magnificent as his own palace. The Marquis must be very rich indeed, he thought, and he gave the hand of his beautiful daughter to the Marquis, then and there. Puss in Boots spread the word to all the lords and ladies throughout the land and they all attended the royal wedding. There was great rejoicing and celebration far into the night, and the Marquis of Carabas and his beautiful Princess lived happily ever afterwards.

Puss in Boots became the Royal Cat and was allowed to do whatever he pleased.

Mr. Bun

AN OLD MAN once said to his old wife, "My dear, I am hungry. Please make me a bun."

"How can I?" she answered. "There is no flour."

"Just scrape the barrel and you will find enough," said the man.

So his wife scraped the barrel and got a bit of flour, which she kneaded into dough with cream. Then she molded the dough, dabbed it with butter and put it in the oven. When it was baked, the wife took the bun out of the oven. It looked delicious, and she put it on the window sill to cool.

Soon the bun began to feel lonely. He rolled off the window sill onto the kitchen floor, and across the floor and out the door. He rolled on down the road and into a field, and there he met a hare. The hare said to him, "Mr. Bun, I shall eat you up!"

"No, please, Mr. Hare, I'll sing you a song if you don't."

He started singing, "I'm Mr. Bun, I'm Mr. Bun. I was kneaded with cream and baked until done. I was put to chill on the window sill, but I got away from Grannie, and I'll get away from you." As he sang his song, Mr. Bun rolled away and disappeared, before the hare could catch him.

T. Tudor

Mr. Bun

He went on rolling until he met a wolf. The wolf said to him, "Mr. Bun, Mr. Bun, I'll eat you up!"

"No, please don't, Mr. Wolf, and I'll sing you a song.

"I'm Mr. Bun, I'm Mr. Bun. I was kneaded with cream and baked until done. I was put to chill on the window sill, but I got away from Grannie, I got away from Mr. Hare, and I'll get away from you!"

He went on rolling across the fields until he met a bear. The bear said to him, "Mr. Bun, I shall eat you up!"

"No, you won't. You couldn't if you tried." And Mr. Bun sang, "I'm Mr. Bun, I'm Mr. Bun. I was kneaded with cream and baked until done. I was put to chill on the window sill, but I got away from Grannie, and Mr. Hare, and Mr. Wolf—and I'll get away from you, too."

He went on rolling further, and met a fox. The fox said to him, "How do you do, Mr. Bun. How nice you look! So brown and crisp-looking!"

Mr. Bun was pleased at being praised. He started singing, "I'm Mr. Bun, I'm Mr. Bun. I was kneaded with cream and baked until done. I was put to chill on the window sill, but I got away from Grannie, and Mr. Hare, and Mr. Wolf, and Mr. Bear, and I'll get away from you!"

"Oh don't go," said the fox. "I'd like to hear that song again, but come closer, please. I'm quite deaf. Come here and sit on my nose."

So Mr. Bun jumped onto the fox's nose and sang his song through again. "Thank you, Mr. Bun," said the fox. "But please sing it just once more, and get even closer. I hear better with my mouth open. Here, come sit on my tongue." The fox opened his mouth and Mr. Bun slid down onto his tongue —and the fox ate him up.

Red Riding Hood

THERE was once a little girl who was loved by everyone, but especially by her grandmother, who could not do enough for her. Once the old lady made her granddaughter a little red hooded cape, and the child liked it so much that she wore it almost all the time. So she was called Red Riding Hood by everyone.

One day her mother called her and said, "Red Riding Hood, I want you to take some fresh bread and cakes to Grandmother. She is not well enough to bake for herself. Besides, it will do her good to see you."

The mother put the bread and the cakes in a basket and covered them with a clean napkin. Then she said, "Go quickly, but do not run or you may stumble and fall on the tree roots in the path. But do not loiter, either."

Red Riding Hood promised she would do as her mother wished, and set out. Now her grandmother lived in the woods, some distance from the village. As Red Riding Hood walked along she met a wolf. She did not know what a wicked beast he was, so she was not in the least afraid.

"Good morning, Red Riding Hood," he said, making his voice sweet.

"Good morning, wolf," she answered.

"Where are you going so early, little Red Riding Hood?"

"To Grandmother's house."

"And what have you in your basket?"

"A loaf of fresh bread and some cakes. Grannie isn't very well and cannot bake for herself."

"That is too bad. Where does your grandmother live?"

"Just at the edge of the clearing," said Red Riding Hood.

The wicked wolf grinned to himself. What a tender little morsel she will make, he thought, smacking his lips. The grandmother will do nicely, too. I'll be cunning and snap them both up!

Then he said, "It is such a beautiful day. There's no need to hurry to your grannie's. Why don't you stop and pick her some flowers? Nothing will please her more than flowers from her little granddaughter."

Red Riding Hood looked about and saw the pretty flowers, and forgetting what her mother had said about loitering, stopped here and there, picking them. The wolf said goodbye softly and trotted off to the grandmother's cottage. He knocked on the door.

"Who is it?" called the grandmother in a weak voice.

"It's Red Riding Hood, Grannie, bringing you fresh bread and cakes," answered the wolf, making his voice small.

"Just press the latch, child," the grandmother cried.

The wolf pressed the latch and pushed open the door. He walked in and before the poor grandmother knew what was happening he opened his mouth and with one gulp swallowed her up. Then he put on a nightgown and cap and got into bed and drew the curtains.

T. Tudor

Red Riding Hood

Red Riding Hood meanwhile picked a big bunch of flowers. Then she came to the clearing and saw that the sun was overhead. It was almost noon! I am very late, she thought, and hurried toward her grandmother's house. How surprised she was to see the door standing open! When she went in, everything seemed strange and dark and silent. Without knowing just why, she was frightened.

"Good morning, Grandmother," she called. But there was no answer.

Then she went to the bed and drew back the curtains. Grandmother was asleep, or so it seemed, and her cap was drawn far over her face.

"Oh, Grandmother, what big ears you have!" cried Red Riding Hood.

"The better to hear you with, my dear," said the wolf, pushing back the cap and looking at the little girl.

"But Grandmother, what big eyes you have!"

"The better to see you with, my dear."

"What big hands you have, Grandmother!"

"The better to catch you with, my dear."

"But Grandmother, what big teeth you have!"

"All the better to eat you with," snarled the wolf.

With that he sprang out of bed and swallowed Red Riding Hood right up. Then he went back to bed, and was soon snoring loudly.

A woodsman passing the cottage heard the snoring and said to himself, "Something must be wrong with old Grannie. I have never heard her snore so loudly. I'll just step in and see if all is well."

So he went into the house and there he saw the wolf fast asleep in the old lady's bed. "You old sinner," said the woodsman. "At last I shall have the pleasure of killing you. You have troubled the countryside long enough, and now your time has come."

He took his knife and slit the hide of the wolf and at once he saw the bright color of Red Riding Hood's cape! After another stroke of the knife out sprang the little girl.

The old grandmother, too, came out alive, though very weak. Red Riding Hood brought big stones with which they filled the wolf, and when he woke and tried to run away he fell down dead.

The woodsman skinned the wolf and took the hide home to make a rug for his hearth. Grannie ate some fresh bread and soon began to feel stronger. As for little Red Riding Hood, she thought, when Mother sends me on an errand and says not to loiter, I never will again!